# The BLIND MEN
## and the ELEPHANT

# THE

A N O L D T A L E

FROM THE LAND OF INDIA

# BLIND MEN

## AND THE ELEPHANT

Re-told by          Illustrated by

LILLIAN QUIGLEY ∷ JANICE HOLLAND

CHARLES SCRIBNER'S SONS · NEW YORK

# NOTE

This is an old fable that children
and grown-ups in India enjoy.

Long ago in India,

six blind men lived together.

Because they lived in India,

they often heard about elephants.

But because they were blind,

they had never seen an elephant.

The blind men lived near
the palace of a Rajah.
The Rajah was the ruler
of all the people.

At the palace of the Rajah,
there were many elephants.
"Let us go to the palace of the Rajah,"
said one blind man.
"Yes, let us go," said the others.

It was a hot day,
but the six blind men walked to the palace.
They walked one behind the other.
The smallest blind man was the leader.

The second blind man put his hand
on the shoulder of the leader.
Each blind man put his hand
on the shoulder of the man in front.

A friend of the six blind men
met them at the palace.
An elephant was standing
in the courtyard.

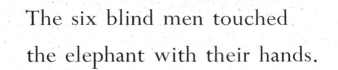

The six blind men touched
the elephant with their hands.

The first blind man put out his hand
and touched the side of the elephant.
"How smooth! An elephant is like a wall."

The second blind man put out his hand
and touched the trunk of the elephant.
"How round! An elephant is like a snake."

The third blind man put out his hand
and touched the tusk of the elephant.
"How sharp! An elephant is like a spear."

The fourth blind man put out his hand
and touched the leg of the elephant.
"How tall ! An elephant is like a tree."

The fifth blind man reached out his hand
and touched the ear of the elephant.
"How wide ! An elephant is like a fan."

The sixth blind man put out his hand
and touched the tail of the elephant.
"How thin ! An elephant is like a rope."

The friend of the six blind men
led them into a garden.
The six blind men were tired.
It was a hot day.

"Wait here. I shall bring you water to drink."
They sat down in the shade
of a big tree.
"You must not go out in the sun
until you rest," he said.
The six blind men talked about the elephant.

"An elephant is like a wall,"
said the first blind man.

"A wall?" said the second blind man.

"You're wrong. An elephant is like a snake."

"A snake?" said the third blind man.

"You're wrong. An elephant is like a spear."

"A spear ?" said the fourth blind man.

"You're wrong. An elephant is like a tree."

"A tree ?" said the fifth blind man.

"You're wrong. An elephant is like a fan."

"A fan ?" said the sixth blind man.

"You're wrong. An elephant is like a rope."

The six blind men could not agree.
Each man shouted.

"A wall !"

"A snake !"

"A spear !"

The friend of the six blind men
came back with water to drink.

At the same time the Rajah was awakened
by the shouting.
He looked out and saw the six blind men
below him in the courtyard.
"Stop !" called out the Rajah.

The six blind men stopped shouting.

They knew that the Rajah was a wise man.

They listened to him.

The Rajah spoke in a kind voice.

"The elephant is a big animal.

Each man touched only one part.

You must put all the parts together

to find out what an elephant is like."

The six blind men listened.
They drank the cool water
as they rested in the shade.
They talked quietly.

"The Rajah is right."

"Each one of us knows only a part."

"To find out the whole truth
we must put all the parts together."

The six blind men walked out of the courtyard.
The smallest blind man led the way.
The second blind man put his hand
on the shoulder of the leader.
Each blind man put his hand
on the shoulder of the man in front.
They walked home,
one behind the other.